P9-DJV-469

GREGORY'S
SHADOW

VIKING · Published by the Penguin Group, Penguin Putnam Books for Young Readers, 345 Hudson Street,
New York, New York 10014, U.S.A.· Penguin Books Ltd, Registered Offices: Harmondsworth, Middlesex, England
First published in 2000 by Viking, a division of Penguin Putnam Books for Young Readers.
10 9 8 7 6 5 4 3 2 1
LIBRARY OF CONGRESS CATALOGING-IN-PUBLICATION DATA · Freeman, Don. Gregory's Shadow / story and pictures
by Don Freeman. · p. cm. · Summary: Gregory Groundhog and his shadow desperately look for each other after they
become separated from one another just before their annual appearance on Groundhog Day.
ISBN 0-670-89328-5 (hardcover) · [1. Woodchuck—Fiction. 2. Groundhog Day—Fiction. 3. Shadows—Fiction.] I. Title.
PZ7.F8747 St 2000   [E]—dc21   00-008205
Printed in Hong Kong
Set in Cooper Old Style

GREGORY'S SHADOW

Don Freeman

Viking

Early one cold morning Gregory Groundhog bundled up before going outside. He had spent the entire winter inside his cozy burrow home. Tomorrow was Groundhog Day. The farmers would want to know if Gregory and his shadow came out of their burrow together. If they did, there would be six more weeks of winter. But if Gregory came out alone, spring would be coming very soon.

"Come, Shadow," Gregory said to his friend. "I can't wait until tomorrow. I'm hungry. Let's go dig up something to eat."

Gregory was shy. Having a friend like Shadow made him feel brave. They did everything together.

"Sure," said Shadow. "I'm right behind you."

Gregory opened the door. It was a windy day but the
sun was shining. The ground was covered with snow.

When the two friends reached the edge of Farmer
Ferguson's garden, Gregory saw another shadow coming
toward him. It was waving its arms. What could it be?

Gregory was frightened. He ran back home.
"Wait for me!" Shadow called out.

But it was too late. Gregory had closed the door. He was
so scared he forgot about his friend. He pulled the covers
over his head and shut his eyes tight. Shadow was left
outside!

Shadow was alone. He was shy, too, and being with
Gregory made *him* feel brave. He looked up from the
shadow with waving arms and saw . . .
Farmer Ferguson's scarecrow.

"Whose shadow are you?" asked the scarecrow.

"I belong to Gregory Groundhog," replied Shadow. "But he left me here. What should I do?"

"I would like to help you, but I don't know how," said the scarecrow. "I don't need a shadow. As you can see, I already have one."

Shadow felt very sad. He leaned against a tree.

"Are you lost?" said the tree. Shadow told her about Gregory. "I would like to help you, but I don't know how," said the tree. "I don't need a shadow. As you can see, I already have one."

"I know where I belong," Shadow said. "With Gregory Groundhog." He walked slowly through the snow.

He soon grew tired. Just then he saw an old barn. "That's a good place for me to rest," he said to himself. "I'll be able to think more clearly after I have a nap." Shadow climbed into the dark cozy hayloft and fell asleep.

Meanwhile, Gregory Groundhog had realized Shadow was missing, and he was hunting for his friend. "Maybe he's under the bed," he thought. But all he saw was the straw mattress he had put there last fall.

"Maybe Shadow is lost," he said. "He must be scared.
I will go find him."

Gregory spent all day searching through the falling snow, and didn't even think about how scared he was. He only thought about finding Shadow.

When it began to snow harder, Gregory ran into the barn.

It was very dark inside.

Bang! The barn door blew shut behind him.

Up in the hayloft, Shadow opened his eyes. He looked down and saw his dear old friend Gregory.

Gregory looked up. He thought he saw something in the hayloft. It looked like a blue ghost!

Gregory was just about to dash out the barn door when
he heard a voice say, "It's me. I'm your lost shadow!"

"Oh, n-n-no you're n-n-not my sh-sh-shadow," Gregory
said. "You're a g-g-ghost!"
Then he ran outside. It had stopped snowing.

Shadow followed his friend into the bright moonlight. Gregory wouldn't leave him behind *this* time!

When Gregory Groundhog turned around he was very surprised.

"Why, you really are my Shadow," he said. "I've found you at last!"

"And I've found you," said Shadow.

Never was there a happier pair.

They danced together far into the night.
Then Gregory said, "I almost forgot. Tomorrow is
Groundhog Day. The farmers will be looking for me."

They made their way back home. "If they see us together they will be unhappy. It will mean six more weeks of winter," Gregory told his friend. He didn't want the farmers to be unhappy. But he didn't want to be separated from his friend again. What should he do?

Early that morning farmers and their families waited to see
the groundhog. They watched from a great distance.

"Here he comes now," said Farmer Ferguson.

Gregory opened the door to his burrow. It was a gray,
cloudy day. He sniffed the air. He saw the farmers. Then he
had a very good idea.

"Hide behind me, Shadow," he whispered.

Shadow understood. He snuggled up behind his friend as
close as he could and held on tight. He was so close no one
could see him!

"Hooray! The groundhog is staying outside without his shadow!" the farmers cheered. "Spring will be here soon. Our hard winter is over."

Farmer Ferguson gave Gregory some delicious vegetables he had kept in his root cellar, to thank him for the good news. And oh, what a feast Gregory had!

Ever since then Gregory Groundhog waits until the second of February to open his door. He and Shadow stay close to each other all the time . . . and they are always *very* brave.